Baby Parade

Rebecca O'Connell   Illustrated by Susie Poole

Albert Whitman & Company
Chicago, Illinois

Here come the babies!
It's a baby parade.

Wave to the baby
in the big red wagon.

Wave to the baby in the soft orange pouch.

Wave to the baby
in the bright yellow
backpack.

Wave to the baby in the bouncy green seat.

Wave to the baby
in the bundle of blue blankets.

Wave to the baby in the purple socks and purple sneakers.

Crawling,

Standing,

Walking!

In the **baby parade**.

To KMW—RO

To the baby safely tucked up in Rachel's tummy! —SP

Library of Congress Cataloging-in-Publication Data

O'Connell, Rebecca
Baby parade / by Rebecca O'Connell ; illustrated by Susie Poole.
p. cm.
Summary: Illustrations and simple text follow babies as they walk, crawl,
ride in strollers, or are carried while enjoying a day with their families.
ISBN 978-0-8075-0509-0 (hardcover)
[1. Babies—Fiction. 2. Parent and child—Fiction.] I. Poole, Susie, ill. II. Title.
PZ7.O2167Bap 2013
[E]—dc23
2012017375

The design is by Nick Tiemersma.

For more information about Albert Whitman & Company,
visit our web site at www.albertwhitman.com.